TIMMY
THE TENNIS BALL

By Abhinav Dinesh
Illustrated by Irvin Ranada

Dedicated to little kids around the world
who love toys, tennis,
and also to my grandparents!

Once upon a time,
there were three tennis ball brothers
living together in a can.
Their names were Rimmy, Jimmy, and Timmy.
The brothers always dreamed
about playing in a tennis game.

After waiting for a long time,
the can was finally opened one day!
The two older brothers Rimmy and Jimmy
were picked up for a tennis game.
However, Timmy was left alone in the can.

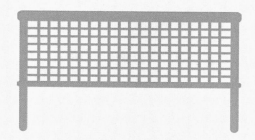

After many days,
it was Timmy's turn to be picked up
for a tennis game.
During practice, he was accidentally hit out
into some big bushes near the tennis courts.

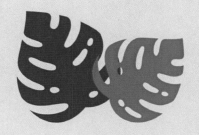

The players went searching for Timmy
but sadly, they could not find him.
Timmy was lost!
For the next few weeks,
it rained a lot and slowly
all his bright colors start to fade.
He wanted to be a good tennis ball
and hoped to play again soon.

One day, Timmy's luck changed
when a little boy named Ravi
came searching for tennis balls to send
to his cousins living in a faraway country
called India.
Ravi's cousins did not have
any toys or balls to play.

While looking under the bushes
near the tennis courts,
Ravi found Timmy all covered in mud.
Timmy was very happy
to have been finally found and lit up
with excitement.

Ravi went home,
carefully washed Timmy with soap,
and dried him to look new again!

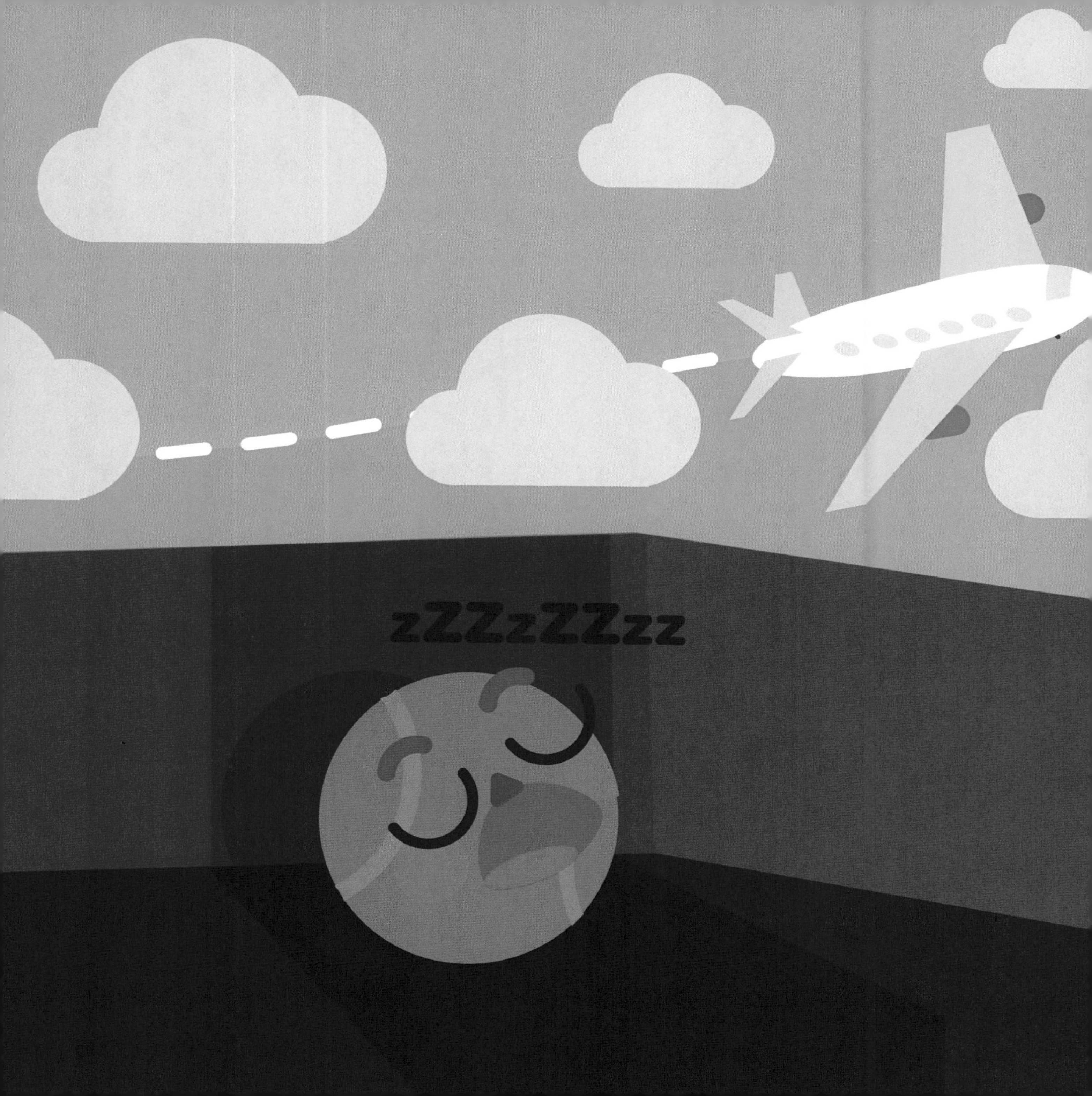
zZZzZZzz

Then he placed him in a box
and mailed it to India.
Timmy felt lonely, scared,
and sad not being able to play,
and fell asleep.

After what seemed like
a long time in the dark box,
Timmy woke up to the sound of laughter
from a little boy and a girl.

When the box was opened, he saw
Ravi's cousins smiling at him.
Timmy smiled back.
The little boy picked Timmy up
and threw him to the little girl
and they ran to a nearby tennis court
to play with Timmy!

Timmy was so happy
that he was finally able to play
in a tennis game.
He realized that he was very special
because the children could play with him,
and he spreads happiness to others!

You too can spread happiness
by sharing your old tennis balls
and toys with other children
who would love to play
tennis or other games with them!

www.happynowfoundation.org

Everyone can make a difference,
and that's what we do at
Happy Now Foundation!
The foundation was started
by the author to collect used tennis balls
in the USA and share them with
underprivileged children
around the world, spreading happiness.

The end of a story,
now let's all begin a journey
to spread happiness!

Made in the USA
Las Vegas, NV
10 March 2024

86966103R00019